W9-BFL-493

Me :"Grandpa, why do you wipe that teapot everyday?"

Grandpa :"This isn't a teapot. It's a magic lamp."

Me :"Aladdin's lamp?"

Grandpa :"Well, whatever! It's the kind where you make three wishes."

Me :"You're kidding."

Grandpa :"When has Grandpa ever lied to you?"

Me: "So what do you wish for?"
Grandpa: "It only works for children."
Me: "So what did you wish for when you were a kid?"
Grandpa: "I wished I would grow up really fast —
and just look at me now!"

I took Grandpa's magic lamp.
He couldn't use it, anyhow.

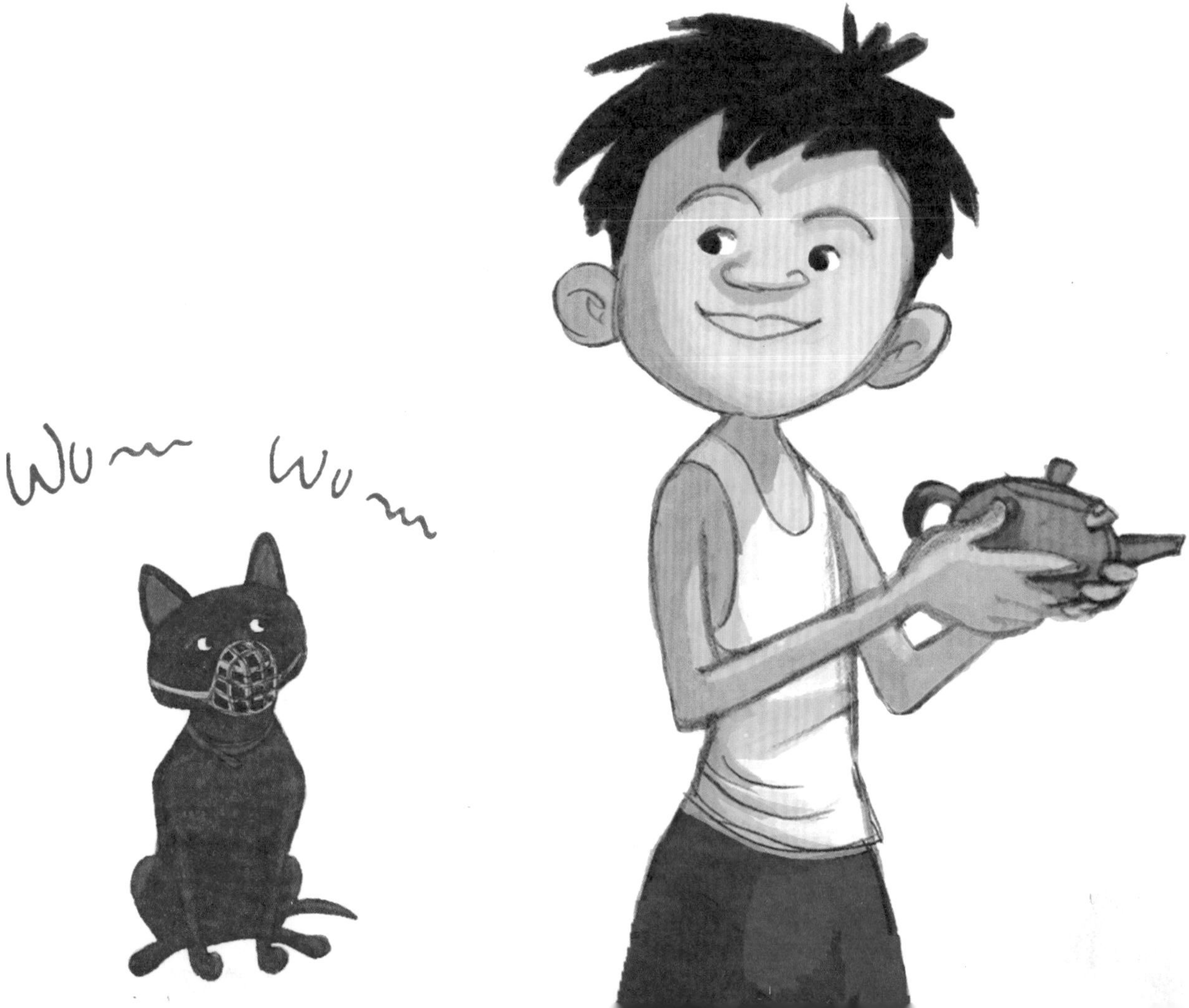
Wu~ Wu~

I was afraid that the genie in the lamp
might make a mistake, so I drew a picture.

My first wish was to get a bike just like this one.

My second wish was to get it very soon.

My third wish...I decided to save that one for later.

I needed some time to think first.

 Books

1033 E. Main St.,#202, Alhambra, CA 91801
editor@heryin.com All rights reserved.
www.heryin.com

Library of Congress Cataloging-in-Publication Data
Ander, 1967- Me and my bike /
written & illustrated by Ander. – 1st English ed. p. cm.
Summary: A child wants nothing more than a new bicycle,
and it seems the wish might come true with some help
from the magic lamp that once made Grandpa grow up really fast.
[1. Bicycles and bicycling–Fiction. 2. Wishes–Fiction.]
I. Title. PZ7.A51875Me 2007 [E]–dc22
2007005817   ISBN : 978-0-9787-5502-7

Me and My Bike

Ander

Heryin Books

Alhambra, California

When I go bike riding with my friends, my mother always tells me not to ride too fast.

I don't ride fast at all. I'm always last.
It's not because I'm a slow rider.
It's because my bike is too big.

Even though they invited me, it feels like my friends

are making fun of me.

They pedal extra fast
so I can't catch up...

And then they have to stop
and wait for me.

They all worry that their bikes will get stolen. I'm the only one who doesn't have a lock.

Wan! Wang!

My parents say how great it is that I can ride such a big bike... then they ask me to carry stuff for them.

This genie is pretty slow.
Why don't I have a new bike yet?

Why am I still on
my Grandpa's bike?

Why hasn't my wish come true?

I dream of my new bike,
even during the day.

The worst thing happened.
My best friend bought the bike.
He must have used the magic lamp
the last time he was at my house.
I should never have told him about it.

I didn't make him fall off the bike –
he just doesn't know how to ride it yet...

My teacher said, we should be happy
to help others. Since my friend can't ride
very well, I'll be his driver.

The magic lamp really works.
We ride together and play together.
Both of our wishes have come true...

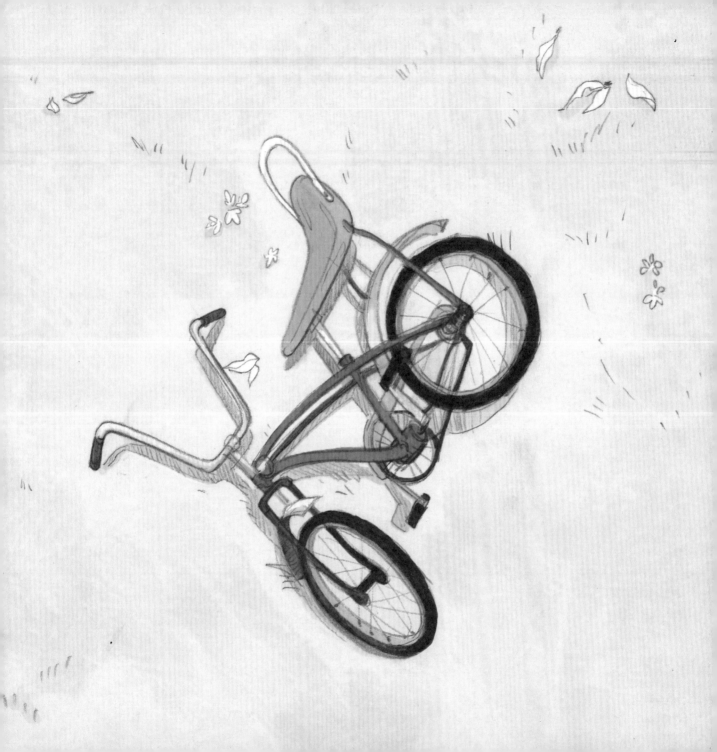

This bike is great.
It's not only fast —
it can be a trail bike, too!

My parents won't let me
ride my friend's bike anymore.

My mom comforts me. She says,
if I get all A's on my next report card,
she'll buy me a bike, too.

Should I use my third wish?

I usually don't even get B's.
This time I study extra hard...
and get straight A's!

I'm afraid my mom will change her mind.
I run all the way home.

Mom looks at my report card and is
just as excited as me! But when I mention
the bike, her smile disappears. She begins
to tell me a story.

She says, when she was small, she had no shoes.
This really embarrassed her, until one day, she
saw a beggar who didn't even have any legs.
Then she knew how lucky she was to be able
to go around barefoot.

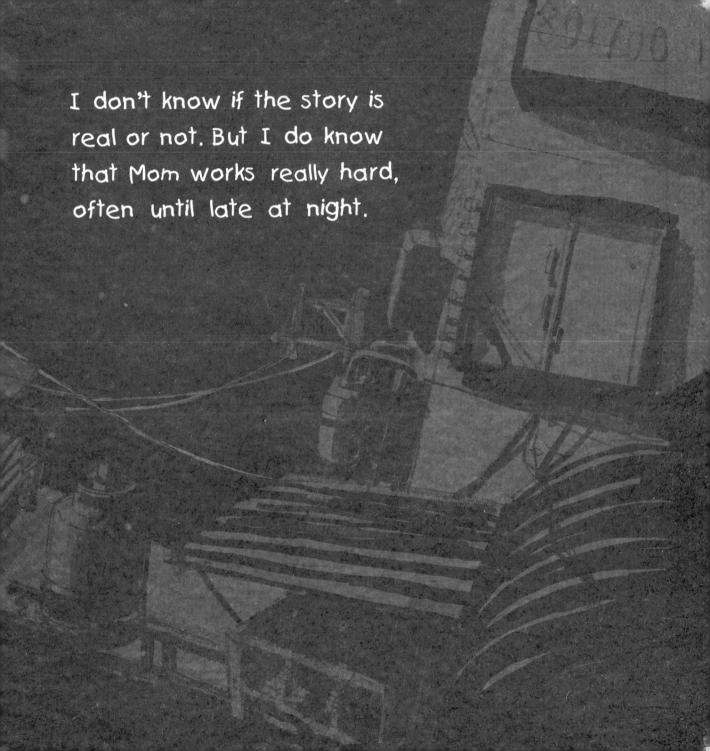

I don't know if the story is real or not. But I do know that Mom works really hard, often until late at night.

I make a decision that amazes even myself. I decide that, instead of a bike, I'll just get some new crayons.

My old bike still works perfectly fine.
If I just give it a new color, it'll look
brand new...

hello!!

And so, now I've got
new crayons and a new bike!

Ok, I'm ready to make my third wish:

I want to grow up fast...
but not get old too soon.